How To Sell Your Sister For Fun and Profit

Written by Ashley Eneriz

Illustrated by Eva Aleph

I dedicate this book to my two daughters, Ellie and Hallie. I pray you will always remember how valuable your friendship and love for each other is.

Hey, you.

Yes, you. Come in close.

A little closer. Perfect!

I've got a good business proposition for you.

Do you want to make
a lot of money?

Do you want to get rid of
that pesky sister once
and for all?

If you answered yes to any of the above questions, then you are the perfect candidate to sell your sister for an amazing profit.

Today, and today only, I am giving away
my best business advice for free.

If you follow these steps closely, you can be on your way
to the bank, while returning to "only child" status.

Step 1:
Make an Attractive Listing.

The first thing you have to do
is make a listing.

For everything else in life, honesty is the best policy.
However, when it comes to selling your sister, you are going
to have to embellish the truth a little.

Don't mention the time she cried for an hour straight in the grocery store or when she broke your favorite toy.

Instead, find a way to flip
the negative into a positive.

Say things like she has
a sensitive spirit and
a special way with toys.

See, no lies here.

Step 2: Add Photos.

To get the most potential profit, you will need good photos. Buyers want to know what they are purchasing before they agree to the deal.

Don't scare off potential buyers with bad photos!

I have found that the most successful sister sales happened with a picture of a sleeping sister.

Step 3:
Set Your Price.

It is always best to start the listing price off a little higher than what you hope to make.

This leaves room for negotiation.

The buyer will feel as if they received an amazing deal
if they are able to get a small discount.

Expect to receive many low offers that do not meet your expectations.
In the business world, it is best to wait for a fair offer.

However, if your sister is being extra annoying that day, then feel free to take any offer quickly!

Step 4: Sign a Contract.

No matter how nice the buyer looks, always have a signed contract.

No returns,

no refunds,

no guarantees.

This will keep you safe
in case they change their mind.

Step 5:
Are You Sure You Want to Sell?

Finally, before you list your sister for sale, make sure that this is really what you want.

It is extremely important to know the future value your sister has. She may not seem worth much now, but she has a huge potential of future worth.

Future things that can make your sister valuable:

Tickle fights

Snuggles
when you are scared

Someone to talk to
when you are bored

A personal cheering squad
at your soccer game

A worthy opponent for
board games

The one person who thinks
you are funny no matter what

Your sister may be hard to live with now, but keeping her around will end up being a worthy investment.

Ten to twenty years down the road, you will be glad you didn't sell her after all.

Made in the USA
Middletown, DE
02 October 2020